You Don't Get to Be a Saint

You Don't Get to Be a Saint

poems by

Patrick Friesen

Turnstone Press

Turnstone Press
607-100 Arthur Street
Winnipeg, Manitoba
Canada R3B 1H3

Turnstone Press gratefully acknowledges the assistance of the Manitoba Arts Council and the Canada Council in the publication of this book.

Cover art: *Anna* (1991) by Esther Warkov, hand-coloured and cut paper collage, pastel, conté, charcoal pencil, 28.5 cm. x 23.5 cm.

Cover photography: Ernest Mayer

Design: Marilyn Morton

This book was printed and bound in Canada by Hignell Printing Limited for Turnstone Press.

Canadian Cataloguing in Publication Data

Friesen, Patrick, 1946-

You don't get to be a saint

Poems.
ISBN 0-88801-163-6

I. Title.

PS8561.R496Y6 1992   C811'.54   C92-098002-3
PR9199.3.F74Y6 1992

Acknowledgements

Some of the poems, or early versions of them, appeared in *Brick*, *CVII*, *Dandelion*, *New Quarterly*, *NeWest Review*, *Poetry Canada Review* and *Prairie Fire*.

anna: A version of this piece was part of a dance collaboration, *Anna*, with choreographer Stephanie Ballard, guest artist Margie Gillis, and dancers Ruth Cansfield, Gaile Petursson-Hiley, AnneBruce Falconer, Odette Heyn-Penner and Faye Thomson. The performance took place at the Gas Station Theatre in June 1987.

My friend Gregory Gendelman told me the fireman anecdote.

singer: Winnipeg blues singer Dave MacLean spoke Manuel's voice wonderfully in the CBC Radio Manitoba production of this piece.

handful of rain: These poems, or versions of them, were part of the Dance Collective production, *Handful of Rain*. This was a multi-disciplinary collaboration with choreographers Ruth Cansfield and Gaile Petursson-Hiley, visual artist Randal Newman, composer Cathy Nosaty, guest artist Maggie Nagle, costume designer Karen Steele and creative consultant Nancy Trites Botkin. Dancers were Kim Knight, Ken Cunningham, Brent Lott, Christina Medina, AnneBruce Falconer and Julia Barrick-Taffe. The performance took place at the Gas Station Theatre in April 1991.

for minnaloushe

Contents

blue flame

anna

first dance

I have sometimes wished at poetry readings that the poet would read a particular poem, or several of them, at least twice. *Anna*, the performance, allowed me to play with the repetition of poems in the second half; adding and subtracting, shifting, interacting with the movements and gestures of dancers on stage. possibly making new poems, or almost new poems, or maybe not. versions. slants. with changes, I do that again here, on the page; the words, this time, on their own.

we walk from streetlight to streetlight
silence to silence
how to speak about the human heart and memory
how to speak about all the rooms we live in

anna akhmatova wrote love poems before the russian revolution. everything changed. her former husband, gumilyev, also a poet, was executed for unspecified reasons in the early '20s. later, their young son was thrown into prison. primarily, it appears, to keep akhmatova silent.

during the '30s a few poems were put on paper, a few of those hand-copied and passed around. mostly akhmatova was silent. in her heart and mind she wrote poems but, for her child, she kept a public silence. these were the years of famine and purges and show trials. akhmatova, along with friends like the mandelstams and pasternak, never knew when stalin would point at her.

after stalin's death, her poems began to appear in publications. strangers often stopped her on the street to thank her for the poems, not only for those few published but for the unwritten ones they knew she had lived. if it's possible for one woman's silence to save the soul of a nation, perhaps a world, this is what akhmatova did. she lived her people's silence, and their poems.

in the later '40s the commissar of culture, let him remain nameless, publicly denounced and ridiculed akhmatova as the "nun and whore" of russian literature. this referred to the fact that akhmatova wrote love poems of several kinds, that she lived and wrote equally in the spirit and the flesh.

akhmatova's silence of the '30s overlaps another kind of silence of the same time. alberto giacometti, who died in '66, the same year as akhmatova, was a swiss sculptor working in paris. for almost a decade he produced next to nothing. each sculpture disappeared. a few small figurines, small enough to fit into matchboxes, survived. giacometti kept sculpting, working toward what he saw, hammering, carving, chipping until there was nothing.

this was a silence. a silence of his materials, if not his process. through the rigours of this merciless vision his famous later sculptures emerged, elongated and thin, almost air. his work was not about objects. they almost disappeared. it was not about society. his work was about itself. his silence was about the act of seeing.

and akhmatova's silences were about being.

how to speak once more about the flesh and the spirit
the red heart and the blue wind

let's say it was 1958 *sail along silvery moon* was on the radio
it was sunday afternoon in july I remember the river and
   swallows swooping low over the water
silver medallions fluttering on their chests the catholic boys
   ran along the springboard and jack-knifed into the seine
   river
there was something ominous about the muddy water like a
   dream anything could be there venomous snakes weeds
   and roots to clutch at you or simply depth something
   ominous and those lean white bodies of faith disappearing
   with graceful dives

I held my breath each time wondering if this one would
drown forever and not return how could he possibly rise
from that darkness of river and overhanging trees how
could the water give him back to light?
but always each boy exploded into air returning from death
or dreams flinging wet hair from his eyes shouting defiance
at the shore and each of us shivering there
and then the sun was so bright dancing in the spray around
the diver's head so bright on his long arms cleaving water
you could hardly believe in anything

let's say it was 1958 I was sitting on the fender of father's blue
dodge and it was sunday and I didn't want to ever leave the
river again

I was eating a persimmon trying to think of God it didn't
work my tongue wouldn't let me get away with it
there are no miracles only mirages in the desert and
disappearances in the river
there's nothing human that isn't betrayed and I know nothing
but what's human my hands my tongue and my face in a
mirror

grandmother wouldn't show me her photographs said I'd
never know what I couldn't would I? her life before me
but I think I remember her in the orchard she was a girl her
hair was soft and flowing down her back her legs brown
with sun

she said sometimes there were angels in the orchard she saw
them among the trees but she wasn't sure and if there were
what should she do?
sometimes there was a black dog or the neighbour's boy with
a stick sometimes there was nothing she could remember
and she was running for her life
this is how she learned to pray she said this is how she
worked her way out her hands at the clothes-line her eyes
on the sky

I don't love the prayer rug obedience or disobedience nothing
that absolute I love the babylonian body and the human
wound I love the surprising word the sinuous approach I
like the world approximately
the way grandfather smoked a cigarette in the garden his feet
lost among the potato plants the way he smiled and I
smelled the drifting smoke his stories hovering among the
raspberry canes the way he leaned on his hoe forever
I love words in the air balanced between mouths and ears I
love the way they're smoke before they're stone
but it's true I think there's not much a voice can say there's a
limit I guess to art there's no end to desire

stepping from shadow I shiver beneath a streetlamp there's
never enough light
I'm waiting for her she'll be wearing black I imagine her
undressing slowly my eyes are raw with looking

I imagine the beauty I see there are such possibilities in these
distances
I almost jump from my skin I want to reach out to what I
imagine

always knocking at the window maybe I'll find myself there
each window a possible mirror
is this eros? longing for consummation in another place on
another day?

I want to break the glass
I want to touch her everywhere

she knows I'm a left-eyed son
seeking an end to memory

she knows I'm an animal of temptations
that I speak out of desire
that I want to disappear at the hem of her flesh

she invites me to read her eyes
I see my hesitation there
on the porch as I reach to knock
and time and again step aside
just when light falls from the opening door

I recognize my pale defiance
I tell her it's all I have
that I don't want a way out
I want to walk in light
I don't want to be caught

she says that somewhere between yes and no
I can answer for myself

that I will end
how my kind ends
looking for other conversations
in other rooms

gregory told a story gregory's from kiev. there was a big fire, a fire so hot no one ventured within a hundred yards of it. barricades were thrown up and firemen tried to get enough pressure in their hoses to reach the distant flames.

the fire was raging out of control everything seemed lost until suddenly a firetruck sped down the street, smashed through the barriers and drove right into the heart of the burning building. a lone fireman leaped from the truck, grabbed a hose and flailed it in all directions. after ten or fifteen minutes the flames died down enough for the other firemen to move in closer and direct their nozzles onto the fire. it wasn't long before the fire was extinguished.

some weeks later a ceremony was held honouring the lone fireman who had courageously doused the inferno. the fire chief, and other dignitaries, praised him fulsomely, and they awarded him $5000. when he handed over the cheque, the chief asked what he would do with the money.

"well," he replied, "the first thing I will do is repair my brakes."

I love her hands the way they touch the garden
I love her hands in water the way they move there or when
 she is silent how they heal
I love how she gathers the world with her hands and lets it
 slip

something about all the rooms I have inhabited the way they
held and released me
rooms that were cloisters or rooms with lamps and seashells
and empty bottles
rooms with pianos or angels rooms where voices died rooms
that were dance-halls for wallflowers

something about rooms the way a room could be a heart filled
with yearning the way the telephone suddenly rang and the
room opened to the world

I remember the night my daughter was born a storm broke all
the windows in the house when I returned home the wind
was blowing through the rooms

rooms of prayer or despair rooms of light

I was standing at the window someone was knocking I went
to the door but no one was there just children laughing
down the street

I was caught in the rain it was the day I knew my death not
everyone's that lucky
everything came together everything was there my footsteps
behind my footsteps ahead my unborn children everything
was there and I knew the number of my days but I lost it
my bones are white it's what I know from grandfather's farm
what's left in the fall scattered bones where horses wheeled
all summer the wind low in the grass and the sudden cold
sweeping rain
I lost everything I thought I was and had didn't have a thing
it was a lie I made didn't know I was that kind of god
didn't know I'd believe my own memory

sometimes it feels like I'm sculpted don't know anymore
who's sculptor who's shaped
like giacometti's figurines not carved from but toward
something I'm sculpted into dust until there's nothing there
or something like nothing
I must think this is some version of divinity what else to call it
there's no purpose here there's nothing to know there's just
this seeing this continual seeing
I must think this is leading somewhere that I am at that
random moment when the chisel can't stop and chips a last
feature into crumbs when I'm plaster dust in the sculptor's
hair or his white footprints on the street

something about the river I heard ice grind in my sleep
something about rivers how they touch what we forget
there's no end to the river where we walk there's no end to
our walk

it doesn't take much a scent of lilacs or rose oil a song it
doesn't take much to remember the world always how it
was the way memory spills through what I see or touch or
hear and there's no end to it like desire

I remember there was no need for the altar icons or text I
didn't know I was being tried
I was barefoot for a moment like grandmother before me
looking for my shoes something to make me human I was
looking for a hat not just any hat my hat I was looking for a hat

memory is a scar I love to touch but will never trust
the future because I was born I trust and can never touch
so I straddle time taking the scraps memory offers and
wanting them again and again

grandmother at the clothes-line the sculptor's baffled hands
   grandfather leaning on his hoe
this is what I know until the end of memory

I walk with her she holds her umbrella above us like a petal
   like ribs holding a heart like the opening cage of the sky
we throw stones into the river we jump pools of water the
   moon's beneath our feet

I was eating a persimmon there's not much to believe or say
   there are mirages in the mirror yes I betray my tongue with
   silence I'm shivering with delight

–what a coincidence.
–what?
–a coincidence. that we met.
–oh.
–reminds me. I heard of a man, somewhere, walking down a street. a baby crawled out a window, fourteenth floor, and fell on the man's head. both survived. a year later, to the day, same man walking down another street. a child leaned against a screen window, fourteenth floor, screen gave way and the child fell on the man's head.
–same man?
–yes.
–same child?
–uh huh. they had moved to a different apartment.
–they lived?
–yes.
–and then?
–and then? that's not enough for you?
–there's always more.

–well, there is. you can imagine the man had problems. his neck was never the same. it wouldn't heal. he visited a chiropractor. thought the receptionist looked familiar.
–it was the child's mother.
–no, no. listen. she looked familiar. he thought he must know her. he approached her and began a conversation. before long they realized they were twins. they had been separated at birth and adopted out. in different cities. let's say their names were bob and linda. well, linda had married a bob and bob had married a linda. they each had two daughters with the same names.
–what about the child?
–the child?
–the one who kept falling on the guy's head.
–oh. well, many years later, the child was a teenager, and the man, bob, was desperately ill and his sister had just died.
–same disease?
–of course. they had both divorced, moved in together, their kids were gone. just brother and sister sharing an apartment, helping each other along. well, she died and he was going fast, so he jumped from a tall building.
–same building where the child fell on him?
–I don't know. he jumped. hit a car stopped at a red light. flew in through the windshield, killed the passenger.
–wait. it was the kid.
–no. the kid was driving. it was the kid's mother.
–you're kidding.
–no.
–could make a person look up now and then.
–that's true. you never know what's going to happen.
–truth is stranger than fiction.
–or life.
–I guess.
–and here we are.
–a coincidence.

–I'm not so sure.
–listen.
–are you adopted by any chance?
–no. listen.
–I knew someone once looked just like you.
–I imagine everyone's got someone looks like them.
–your name. you must have a name.
–I'd rather not.
–let me guess.
–I won't tell you.
–well, then, I'll guess what your name isn't.
–listen, I've got to go.
–george.
–I'm not saying.
–lenny.
–listen.
–albert.
–I'm going.
–emile. frankie. vincent.

anna

second dance

after stalin's death, strangers often stopped akhmatova on the street to thank her for her poems, not only for those few published but for the unwritten ones they knew she had lived. she had lived her people's silence.

akhmatova's silence overlaps another kind of silence of the same time. alberto giacometti sculpted, working toward what he saw, hammering, carving, chipping until the material crumbled and there was nothing.

his work was not about objects. it was not about society. his work was about the act of seeing, about trying to show us what he saw.

akhmatova's silences were about being, until the day she could pull down the words and help us remember.

silver medallions fluttering on their chests the catholic boys ran along the springboard and jack-knifed into the seine river

always each boy exploded into air returning from death or dreams shouting defiance at the shore

and the sun was so bright dancing in the spray around the diver's head so bright on his long arms cleaving water you could hardly believe in anything

there are no miracles only mirages and disappearances

sometimes there were angels in the orchard grandmother saw them among the trees but she wasn't sure and if there were what should she do?
she learned to pray she said her hands at the clothes-line her eyes on the sky

I don't love obedience or disobedience nothing that absolute I like the world
grandfather's stories hovering among the raspberry canes
I love words in the air balanced between mouths and ears I love the way they're smoke before they're stone

I shiver beneath a streetlamp there's never enough light
I'm waiting for her I imagine her undressing slowly my eyes are raw with looking
I want to touch her everywhere

I love her hands in water
I love how she gathers the world with her hands and lets it slip

something about all the rooms I have inhabited

rooms with broken windows rooms of rain

I was standing at the window someone was knocking

caught in the rain it was the day I knew my death

I lost everything didn't know I'd believe my own memory

I must think this is some version of divinity there's no
purpose here there's nothing to know there's only this
seeing this continual seeing

listen, a sculptor was dying; I don't remember his name. he was spanish, an atheist. the town priest heard and hurried to the death room with a crucifix. the room was simple and bare. the dying man lay near an open window.

"now my man," said the priest, "for that is all you are, a man. now as you face the vista of eternity, as you face judgement and flames, you who have denied Him so long, always saying 'no', who have proudly walked on the human road, won't you look once upon Him before your eyes close forever, won't you look once upon your God and submit?"

the sculptor opened his eyes to the familiar crucifix.

"I have. I made him."

the story proves nothing. like all stories, it is. words become stones.

the future, because I was born, I trust and can never touch. so I straddle time, taking the scraps memory offers and wanting them again and again.

I'm a left-eyed son
seeking an end to memory

somewhere between yes and no
I answer for myself

I stand in the doorway
and end how my kind ends
looking for other conversations in other rooms

starry night

starry night

frankie's heading for the country last chance for love nothing
  but blowing snow and cold a quarter moon hanging like a
  scythe and nothing's doing driveways drifting no light
  anywhere just frankie's numb foot on the accelerator and
  his eyes on the vanishing road
you can't lose what you haven't got frankie he knows there's
  nothing he owns that's how it goes he knows he came alone
  and that's how he's going
frankie's gnawing his nerve somewhere there's a song lost in
  the eaves or down the well frankie's trying to sing
but everything floats away the road beneath him the song
  frankie can't believe a thing the windshield's frozen with
  stars
he's got the ache it's what you earn alone frankie's got the
  terror tonight the sky has no eyes and snow splinters the
  headlights

lost the answers long ago been clinging to last things the old
  nag and windmill been clinging to god's blue umbrella
don't always know who's speaking frankie's on the road he's
  cold don't always know who's listening tonight there's no
  warmth there are such nights a woollen scarf a cloak and
  nothing ever warm again
there are slow nights of dread teeth chattering at dawn when
  eyes encounter the world raw
sometimes the ventriloquist moves his lips you turn but you
  can't find the words
I've seen the sky riddled with holes and seething stars I've
  seen the steeple
don't want deception no more light bells are tolling in town
  someone's down the night's dark and no one's hanging on

let's go crazy frankie give me a silver ring I'll pay your way
  let's take a chance we'll go sailing and float our hats
come back frankie come on home we'll shake a bottle at the
  moon until everything goes
I've had my times been a fool on horseback a broken window
  for the sun I've slit my throat for words walked water with
  the gypsy
I've loved the only rose how else to say it I've leaned on the
  balcony watching long light inside the trees
I've learned the ropes my hands are free let's go crazy frankie
  there are the children there's you and me

day breaks with ice on the anvil the cat's licking frost from her
  feet frankie's home
day breaks like eternity this is how we live all the balls in the
  air and no one to catch them
feels frankie like we're alone here beyond bewilderment and
  short of paradise
I've had the jitters tonight been dreaming the soft shoe but the
  dance floor's deserted door's open and shivering on its
  hinge
don't ever say goodbye frankie wait for the bluff somewhere
  the dancer draws a ribbon from her hair she's got one foot
  in the rain one foot on the stair

blue shoes *for margie*

in the hottest summer alive with the sky appallingly blue and
blind guilt burned out like a house on stilts
in the collapsed porch in everything that can't be retrieved or
forgotten in the peeled paint on the wall
in the memory of the spear flying through childhood in
hallowe'en masks in blue shoes walking relentlessly toward
an end

when you're wide open with need when you call for someone
and you become a naked voice bare of nuance and finesse
of memory when you can't help yourself and you call
when you're a drum waiting to be struck a stage ready to be
danced when you're at the mercy of love
when you're terrified when you shiver because you've been
flayed when you laugh or cry at the drop of a hat when it's
your hat
when you feel your way toward the frost and desolation of
windows and just the possibility of a window where you
can rest without bags and shoes without everything you
have to do and be
when you move toward freedom meeting its necessities with
hands up when you hear wind on the roof and you're
expecting rain when you loosen and billow like a sail

someone in the world turns toward you and you've been
found and you give up
someone unbuttons you and washes your body the heaviness
lifts and because she has consented to be your need and you
become hers you are two children talking late and laughing
as if this is really how things happen
someone holds you for a moment at the foot of the stairs she
offers her window and you believe nothing because
everything's true your fingers on her collar-bone and she
leans to touch the light in your feet

it's impossible though after brilliant days of waking after
tenderness and gestures of affection
it's impossible how love like imminent death shows us the
river or tree for a first time and like death shuts our eyes
again
it's impossible love's bafflement as it turns a corner how we
return to our ordinary rooms how memory is a slow
assassin
it's impossible how we pass time a pair of shoes at the door
it's impossible the commotion of another birth

irish lullaby

I've been swaddled with fear seen black crows in the field
  everyone's got a dark window at home
I've been wearing hallowe'en shoes a long time I've been
  drunk with october fire
there's a cold moon on the back porch tonight there are
  prayers that got nowhere and trees are barbed wire against
  the sky
someone's howling could be from the catacombs or my
  dreams of snow could be a memory of wings an assault on
  heaven could be a boy's dream of thunder
someone's licked the edge of the moon and I wonder where I
  was last night when it fell

I was swilling *wray and nephew* it almost gave me religion at
  two a.m. nijinsky loose and sword dancer on the run again
I was drinking toward closing time when the extravaganza
  ends and words drift away on the street and you're
  stumbling home with an irish lullaby in your ears
a boy calls for mother so does a man who doesn't when the
  wind blows sudden or the rope gives way
a boy jumps cracks in the sidewalk it doesn't matter nothing
  changes and somewhere the street ends

a boy's bereft they're starving in china ma said me wanting
everything that's how it used to be
every one of me stood up for execution I asked for a last drink
and another I had the thirst it happens drinking into desire
someone had to find the end of the road
ma said I could lose my eyes or drown and no witnesses
anything could happen I wanted anything to happen
sometimes a boy's bereft a priest in the rain a diver caught in
air
I remember each drowning pale boys sinking in the seine or
faltering alone in the sand pits I've seen their loose-limbed
bodies sagging beyond hands and hooks I've seen them
fatherless in the river

I wanted to drown from too many angels there are no
companions in paradise I wanted to drown again in the
world
I met gypsy in the fall I climbed a mountain ash for berries
and I gave them to her gypsy's silver bracelets shivered in
the dark she walked lanky her ankles bound in scarves
I was dangerous on the hill but gypsy laughed and moved
close for warmth she knew this kind of heat and she'd been
cold
sometimes you slip the tyranny of fear at night and the world
shines beneath your feet sometimes you shake loose and
gypsy's in your arms

dreaming the dolphin

frankie's got birth and love and god frankie's got the usual
wounds he's lost the deftness the gifts of grace what it takes
to heal
frankie's got defeat in his eyes today he's got fatigue frankie's
got fungus and parasites frankie's feeling sorry for himself

frankie's the joker you can't take home no one wants to die
laughing he's a gossip at the fence a flame no one doused a
hazard a heat some kind of light
frankie love the wound he knows night frankie kiss the hand
but frankie's gone looking for zero he's looking for the
goose egg frankie's got to find the silence

frankie's got lilies he's got irish memories and *tura lura*
frankie's dreaming the dolphin
frankie's a trapeze for angels he's sheet music he's the
juggler's hands frankie's the words for a prayer he'll never
say

a woman from jamaica *in memory of geita forbes*

I don't think it's too much to ask that for a moment every
wound heal and stutter toward silence
I don't think it's too much to ask for a hesitation of the
highball thundering through our veins
let's say we can halt fear let's say this room is enough that all
streets and rivers flow here that all gods drink at this bar

I know a woman from jamaica who tells annancy stories she's
laughing like a mischievous child
I know a woman who could outleg the obeah man and she
has who could walk water and she will
tonight's her final dream what each of us will dream the
world loosening and shifting like catastrophe but it's only a
single death

is the music loud enough can you hear it on your skin?
are the chairs and tables dancing is the dolphin diving in?

a woman is dying when she takes my hand I feel the chill of
the cold mirror she has held
a woman is dreaming annihilation hands reaching and
rapacious wicked hands that harass her they want to break
the mirror she raises it high above them with her thin arms
she knows what this is this encounter with the end she has
never stood a longer night
when it's over she says when jehovah's come and the mirror
whole she'll see what is left her long body in death she'll
know she was here in this blue place of water and grass

is the dream loud enough can you feel it on your skin?

a dying woman has climbed out of the dark agitation of
prayer and terror with the ghost in her hands
a woman is walking by the water she leaves her shadow and
the willow a woman is rowing away
I don't think it's too much to ask that for a moment every
wound heal and stutter into silence
let's say we can halt fear let's say the music's loud enough we
can hear it on our skins and the chairs are dancing the
dolphin's diving in

killing time

after the funeral we talked about next of kin and blood aunt
martha said it was thicker than water you had to stick with
yours
catholics drank it said uncle john and lutheran farmers ate
blood sausage their cats lapping it from buckets beneath the
stuck pig hanging by its hocks

rosie thought she was dying when she bled and her just
thirteen and happy the moon was on the mare she said
laughing with a sigh
milton tasted his blood like all children ever he died of it
lawrence spat his the world hemorrhaging from his ears
and nose

I was thinking of blood the fetish and sacrifice lamb or christ
the virgin heart held aloft and still beating to the sun
I was thinking icons and blood baths on the border I was
thinking disease and prayer and copulation seemed all the
same and earth taking it in

always killing time somewhere in the sinks and hills and
altars blood exploding in great gobs at paschendaele or the
mission field
fat or thin always somebody hungry uncle john joking I
should try blood pudding to give me colour could make a
man lose faith there's always thirst

aunt martha said she'd dreamed it flowing through the great
rift of africa leaving nothing but bones and stone uncle john
thought he'd heard it in the dark angel's trumpet
I was remembering my children the rainstorm bursting at
birth the human heart a bag of blood hanging by a thread

aunt martha insisted everything happened twice if you lived long enough like living in front of a mirror rosie asked why twice seemed to her there was no end to it didn't matter how long you lived
rosie loved the sea said it was a place you could forget you were human uncle john agreeing sometimes you just had to be yourself

my hand on the doorknob I was thinking there's so little blood to see where does it go you'd think we'd be choking on it you'd think we'd never be clean again
I was looking for the way out uncle john asked why not stay for lunch and aunt martha smiling with her long white teeth said come again for carnival

hallowe'en woman

I was born in the leaves and commotion of grandmother's
garden in the memory of the angel passing through
I was born where the heart begins imagine it red as a rose or a
small violence at the wrist imagine it in love or at the end of
its rope

I was breathing someone else's breath I don't know how it
happens this overlapping of lives these dreams of life
I heard the sucking child the doctor at the door I heard the
songs of europe and blackbirds in the reeds

anna walked through town with her bastard son she washed
everyone's floors and clothes anna was the sin of the world
the gamble of desire and its scandal
anna couldn't help winking it was something outside
laughter she couldn't help the wind she couldn't move the
river

anna walked through her garden the earth beneath her nails
she stooped to stroke the cat and always in the fall she built
fire
everyone has many hearts she said adore them each and let
them go this is how the world slips by in its rapture and
misery

I remember her mischief how she ridiculed the world with
her tricks and glee I remember her gifts of glass and cloth
anna was the hallowe'en woman in her ancient dress she
knew the cruelty and pleasure of children she had the wits

anna told me something about love that it's lightning in the
hand a river a disease she told me it's something human at
best
each terror hesitates she said when you love there's no fearing
beauty or pain or power when you love someone you are
irresistible

I live in anna's garden in its excavations I wonder why I keep
digging for words I think it's about the usual things the
pool stirring or first light it's about the hand in water and
the flesh of god's other face
I live in the scent of an embrace grandmother in her flowered
dress anna with her sweet breath

in the end it's all for her my blind words lurching I hope
toward the angel in the end it's all for her gamble and her
unjudging arms
I keep a room for her a wooden chair and a bed I keep candies
in a bowl near the door the last heart is a bright pocket of
seeds the last heart is a chinese lantern hanging from its
stem and all around the garden's smoke

dream of the world *for marijke and nikolaus*

there is a dream I have of anna in the doorway this is almost a
memory of july a handful of clouds drifting in a monet sky
and anna's sudden silhouette
this is a moment when I know everything when school is out
and I'm dreaming irish this is when the world ignites in my
eyes

there's a story where I'm prowling in the kingdom looking for
shade I was wild once in my head I was wild in my heart
someone slipped through the garden's green and hoe I was
coughing in a bush a suicide of leaves I had the sky and
hawk I got gladiators on the brain

there is a dream where I'm drunk beside the road or it's father
one of us at the end of himself there are black trees in april
and I can't see the wind anywhere
this is a memory of sun and a consolation of shadow this is a
day of keening and love and the end of fathers

it's a memory me praying the way children play me looking
east and west nothing there nowhere nothing is never
something nothing is what you breathe when god's on fire
there is a dream of empty pockets where I can't find my
hands there is a dream where anna steps smiling from the
door and I fly into another dream of the world

lions and blasphemy

feels sometimes like a tin whistle like cirrus clouds shifting
  across july feels like the imp at the river
feels like morning clothes hanging from a willow feels like
  gooseberries like the ghost or something singing in the reeds

feels like speargrass or stone or ploughed earth feels like
  thistles through an iron wheel
feels like sun through the windshield like blowflies and the
  radio feels like voices from the trees

feels like church or the body's wordless pain feels like noon
  like yellow fields and crows
feels like water the mariner's story feels like drowning feels
  like the lake's serenity

feels like the empty cradle or still leaves no one breathing
  feels like the blue bottle tumbling through air
feels like a house like bare windows and stairs feels like
  moonlight across the narrow bed

feels like lions and blasphemy like uilleann pipes like
  laughter like spitting on the grave
feels like scarves and wind like dogwood feels like ruins and
  rain and nothing to wear

black cat poem

I've been dreaming snow and streetlamps and sent the singer
home I've been growing thin on a narrow bed but tonight
the moon's in the window and black cat's on the sill
some rooms can't tell lips from hands or words from love
some rooms are lost in the city of memory this room can't
tell door from walls
yesterday I had the sadness in my eyes tonight I taste her on
my tongue she shows me the river where tall women live
she walks there in silk and scarves

I believe almost nothing but I do believe in gifts grace some
call it or miracle I believe nothing but hand finding hand
black cat arches her back and steps from the sill there are
passions not meant for words she breathes at my throat or
bites my lip sometimes there are no choices and we choose
each other
this room empties when we love slipping away but the room
knows us well that we will return like all lovers to our skins

the girl from botany bay *for trites*

a woman has come from far she has brought her shore and
stones she has brought the wildness of a girl
I almost can't kiss her she's moving so quickly through her
life she touches me with her hand or voice then she's gone
sometimes I see the trouble in her eyes she's standing at the
window with moon on the snow she longs for danger
she holds a memory of love still raw and brutally beautiful
she opens her hand slowly and turns toward the girl

I want to know the girl she was on the beach before men
before she left the back door and stepped into the bare-
legged sea
I want to know when everything was slow her walking
through the whole day singing *let me call you sweetheart*
I want to know eucalyptus and choir everything she smelled
or heard in july I want to know the stones she carefully
gathered in her skirts the gulls marauding her hair
I want to know the way she shoved her hands into her
pockets the day she knew who she was and spun from her
father's call
I want to know her delight with the world how she loved
wind on her neck I want to know her leaning against the
sky before she left the girl and feared

I must have dreamed her drowning her walk into the sea I
know the gathering of light and dark into her only choice
she has come from the child's shore and a woman's despair
she has died calling the empty names she has reached an
end to prayer
there is no one to tell her how one love can destroy another
she has bearded God the name and hazarded her life she
has come through questions and found more
I can't love her enough and I won't I will love her this is all
she wants from me she's turning toward the wild girl and
the shore

the silence of angels

a girl returns from the sea with a basket of sand and her doll
  she breathes easily each breath a small warmth in air
a barefoot girl walks through the forbidden places she's a fish
  and a bird she's stone three ways of knowing

there are no ghosts in the tree and nothing around the bend
  this is the silence of angels the meantime between words
a girl moves through her skin like light on water she sings to
  her morning star and enters rain as if it's dreaming her

a girl loves her toes in earth the road disappearing toward
  what she doesn't know herself remembering this first child
she can't tell the day or hour all that's left is what's there
  leaves on both sides of the road the sky open like a sea

her eyes rupture the world by seeing her voice singing or
  muttering to itself splinters into stories
a girl walks with herself down the road she knows calling on
  the other side of silence

each moment there's a hole where she was but it heals each
  moment the air rifts then knits together behind her
a girl walks around the bend with a basket of sand and her
  doll the road does not remember her feet

first step into air *for per (out of our conversations)*

a man leans out a window looking up and down the street for
 a familiar shape someone who just passed someone he
 might remember
sometimes it's a voice through the door half a conversation he
 once had or a song from the sea
he turns suddenly because there's someone behind him he
 almost knows who but it's only something ordinary like
 leaves rustling at the wall

a man stands at the railing of a bridge he's father and son he
 wants the river he wants the sky a man stands between
beneath this bridge is where lovers preen and children play
 this is where we spread our blanket
a man follows his shadow through the end of the day he's
 yearning for a body his if he can find it hers if that's where
 it is

he remembers mother's arm curved around him and the
 absence on the other side he remembers every song she sang
he knows the ballads and lullabies that made him prince or
 drowned man he knows the hymns of heaven
a man recalls his birth dazzling light on the harbour his proud
 father baffled in the tavern there is an embrace he needs

a man can't reach as far as he wants and reaches too far he
 feels flayed sometimes all bones and height and nothing to
 touch
grief is the word for this or grieving but his fumbling with the
 doorknob and the empty room where love lived there are
 no words for that
what can't be said has something to do with a man's first step
 into air it has something to do with mourning

feels we're near tears shivering and short of breath it's cold
near the window and the air is thin
a man sits on his empty suitcase in an empty house he's not
leaving this is an exile's return
we forgot we had these tears pain blossoms like an opening
fist the heart demands its reparation

he keeps turning because there's nothing ahead always the
voice is from behind and someone's tugging at his coat
there's a nagging almost a word on his tongue as if he's
already said it yet he's only about to speak
he leans into the rain to watch the faces pass he listens to the
singer on the street a man no longer answers to his names

singer

the late richard manuel was pianist, occasional drummer and one of the vocalists in that remarkable rock group, the band. his was the first voice I heard when I purchased *music from big pink* in 1968 and placed it on my turntable. I loved his voice immediately.

after manuel's suicide in 1986, I found myself mulling over the few details I had learned of his life; details and their relationship to his voice. I wondered what his inner conversation had been at the end; his conversation with himself and with his muse.

I wrote a radio piece for voices: my mulling and his imaginary conversation.

Voice 1:

I've always been fascinated by voice   what it is   where it comes from   how it is silenced   voice as utterance and as something before and after utterance   I'm fascinated by the physical voice, a strumming in the throat, how it can sound the heart

one of the voices that came through for me was that of richard manuel   there was pain in his life, there was joy   you could hear it

Voice 2:

seems an impossibility   that someone can make a song   out of nowhere   what are the odds?

I don't know where she comes from   been around a long time   she wants too much   sometimes I have to shake her   do one thing or another so I can forget

but she always shows up   reminding me   I'll be driving through the night, forgetting, following the white line   and she's there, caught in my headlights

I close my eyes   when I open them, she's still there   when it's too much, sometimes, I gun the car at her   but always I swerve at the last second   or she dances aside

Voice 1:

the band was amazing   cowboys and blues singers with some gospel to boot   three unique voices harmonizing, overlapping, trading off   it felt like family   just how it goes around the piano   no posturing or self-indulgence, no production getting in the way   everything sounded loose, even sloppy, yet this was the tightest band I'd ever heard, quirks, raw edges and all

there was yearning in manuel's voice   something lost in his falsetto   sometimes he sounded tired   always it was a voice that sounded like itself, if that makes sense

it was a voice I never doubted

Voice 2:

this is how it happens

sticks in my hands   I hesitate   lost between beats   there's tension   like looking down from a tall building   you know you're going to fall, you can't resist   it's terrifying, but you want what you fear

you can't save yourself   someone's got to reach out and break the spell   someone's got to grab you   a touch, and you shiver back into your skin, like the crack of a drum out of silence

you've got to find your way back

Voice 1:

manuel was born in canada   stratford   don't know much about the town   someone told me there were swans and ghosts   it made sense   I imagined victorian eccentrics drifting down the sidewalks   wondered how a spanish name like manuel found its way into town

he played in bands early   friends called him *beak* because of his nose   eventually he joined ronnie hawkins, along with the other guys   they split, found their way down the back roads of the southern states   they became dylan's band on the way to the big time   and then they were just the band

a short way to say a lot happened   all background, a context, something to shape a voice

Voice 2:

I don't understand this craziness   what was dealt

don't know if I built this myself, or was I born into it   how I can't do what I need to do   the restlessness, but nothing happens   just waiting for someone to take me in hand   I'm not what I seem

you get older, everything gets more necessary   everything gets more impossible

there's too much world, and the words don't come

look at her   she's old, she's waiting   in all the years, the betrayals, she's never been this old   nagging

Voice 1:

manuel's voice had all the elements   it was raw, like a bare wire

how to put it   that words played a part but didn't matter in the end   what mattered was the singing itself, how his tongue curled around the words

it's how you take what you are and have from birth, how you find out what you almost know, what you need to know, how you make something that's not been heard before

a voice

how your voice is soaked with experience   not necessarily a long life of events, but what you were born, the angels who came in with you   you've got to live them, you've got to give them their place   they are yours, they are you

some people are singers   some of them sing for the rest of us

truth is not a word you can trust, but you've got to accept something behind the word   the human need to be touched and to know when you have been touched   no questions asked

there's more than one way to train a voice   its relationship to the note or how it bends the note or perhaps finds another side to the note   sometimes you have to sing between the notes   or hold the silence

manuel didn't interpret songs   his voice was the song   he possessed it, as if he'd written it   you were hearing it for the first time because it was always the only time for him

Voice 2:

it was like cinema, this dream   one thing after another   I remember a couple of scenes

a man is breaking rocks   the sun glinting off the hammer as he swings and swings   never stops for a rest   all day   finally, the sun sinking, he stops and turns to me, says he's got to get through this mountain of rocks to find his name   he's got to earn a name

later, he's fishing with a friend   they're in a boat   he's drunk and falls overboard, but there's no splash and he can't drown because he's already drunk

his friend falls in too, but he's drowning because he doesn't remember his name

I don't know

I guess you can dive into any water as long as you know your name

Voice 1:

all artists mess with silence, some are caught in it

what the wound was that silenced manuel I don't know   he always seemed defenceless, too open, as if he took everything to heart   one of god's own children

apparently he couldn't write songs by the third album whatever he had to say, he couldn't say it   not with words   he must have fought with the angels   often he sought refuge in cocaine and drink   who knows what's cause and what's effect?

when he sang it was a kind of haunting, the singer and the song   you couldn't always tell which was in control   who haunted whom?   you heard the wound in his voice, the texture   and the silence his voice broke

sometimes I feel haunted by his death   his own hand after long silence, hanging by his belt in some motel, not desperate but tired   as if it was all decided long ago   returning to his ghost

sometimes a voice breaks through the spells

Voice 2:

what the hell

I'm always spilling something   the *grand marnier* knocked over   my house of cards   the notes   always something spilled and nothing to sop it up

the hand trembles or the eyes turn in   something spills, you'd think the room would be a river

just looking in the mirror   watching the flames dance   but there's nothing in front of the glass   watching the flames and trying to foot it through the night

such a strange dance

everything spilling

I've never known a colder room or an emptier door

handful of rain

silence

if it's chosen
silence is not an enemy
it is where words begin and end
silence is the heart's chamber
between beats

lost boys

one moment the silence of trees
the next a cacophony of macaw and monkeys
boys of leaves hanging by their knees
taunting the sky and laughing
a kind of raucous worship

it's the stillness I wonder about
the memory behind their eyes
I wonder what their bodies know
lost between the kingdom and the abyss

a dream of mothers

I used to reach for her hand in church the sermon droning
around us I loved to touch her hand in the heat tracing her
long fingers measuring my hand in hers
the coolness of her fingers on my fever I used to clutch her
hand as I rode the waves of delirium an anchor and a vow

I remember her carrying my sister she took my hand and held
it to her belly I remember the taut skin the pure and hard
curve beneath my palm
I remember from a dark hallway seeing her step back from
the cupboards one hand to the small of her back a strand of
hair she tucked in with the other

I reached for her hand in a storm my eyes shut and rain
washing across the window I felt her heart at the wrist
become a quiet thunder
sometimes wondering who she was she said I had her hands
sometimes I was an orphan lost in a dream of all my
mothers

when I close my eyes I see her on her knees cupping holes of
earth in her hands and releasing seeds from her mouth who
could offer such burials
I know her voice the whole sung and spoken world across the
table or through the kitchen screen who could ever kiss an
ear like that

rowing home

sundays after a week of the hammer after ladders and beams
and skyline father collapsed in a sprawl like an idling motor
about to stall like a tamarack leaning into fall like a bundle
of clothes or a doll
it frightened me as if he was dying as if the strength of his
arms was flowing through his fingers into air as if the
continent of his body was sinking away as if his breath was
a sigh from the end of the world
I watched the hesitant rise and fall of his chest I imagined his
red heart slow-pulsing the blanket slid from his shoulders
and he turned against the cold reaching blindly in his sleep
for comfort
he seemed a wounded lord I wanted to bury his name take
him into my arms and carry him to the river to find the boy
he was I wanted to row him home

black umbrella

street's empty
window's bare

where are you?

there's smoke on the lawn
an empty suitcase on the porch

sometimes I turn at a sound
from the corner of my eye
I think I see a red shoe holding the door ajar

and I hear a breathing

where are you
with your danger and your smile?

I wish I could step into someone's shoes

I listen to trains all night
with a telephone cradled at my ear
I can smell your skin

where are you?

I don't know myself anymore
drowning at the window
water closing over my head
my feet feeling for the emptiness beneath me
this is the last place my body knows before it surrenders

where are you?
wandering the beach beneath your black umbrella
naked and looking for clothes
come for me I will be your dress

sometimes my hands hardly remember the world

sometimes my hands hardly remember the world

silk

a son's tears

the nape of my lover's neck
beneath her hair

my hands
in greeting
or at the typer

sometimes my hands are widowers
without a world to touch

sometimes I love the simplicity of snow
its sensuality at twilight
its comfort on the windowsill at night

a stray

I was ten my hair soaking wet and water running down my
neck
I was ten my feet in a pool and me clutching my pantlegs at
my knees

I knew who I would be

I was shivering from rain from knowing
a handful of water trickling through my fingers

mother taught me the syllables
father the sums

I guess I lay down with the moon
fire leaping high
I guess I was a stray

a restless creature
neither demon nor saint
never dressed for the occasion

someone always calling
and no one ever there

this restless creature
standing in the rain

I was young my heart wild and bare
I spun around on my toes
my arms flying out for something to embrace

before syllables and sums
before love

I knew I was a stray

blue flame

blue flame *for nancy*

sometimes silence is sultry a restless heat and a gaping for
breath sometimes it's a drone at the window and crawling
skin
there are days when light leaves the animal's eyes and leaving
the door it drags its belly beneath the house
there are no lamps or rings no spells to say only the word that
will not come
she knows words like breathing she knows the silence that
takes breath away there are no choices to be made

this cage is hard as flesh a blue flame beneath the skin and
paper's white waiting on the desk
day after day she rummages at the keys for just a little music
but all she finds is fear
each day slips away with random gestures the washing of
windows the broom's work the forgetfulness of eating
nothing happens and nothing changes but her darkness is
always as near as the mirror
something sifts through her fingers sun dust or words
something passes and nothing's left to lose

it's in the waiting buried in the stifled corners of waiting that
  something shifts for a moment the curtain sways a shadow
  lengthens on the wall
she feels it inside her body an unclenching a small pain
  something of her own a birthmark she feels the animal
  stretch and shake off its death once again
the fox at her door deep-chested pelicans at anchor these are
  words standing on the beach in her footprints this is an
  unearthing of words
but to speak them is impossible she knows this she works
  only with echo with mimicry this effort of words is an
  empty room with a thousand windows
this is all the only salvage of waiting imprecise words the
  song you hear when you tilt your head someone humming
  behind you

fox

when the sun is high in the still afternoon when you turn
from your desk to stretch and gaze out the window she is
there
the gift of a fox how she keeps a distance yet meets your eyes
intimately from the edge of the clearing
a small fire a moment of light nothing is as awake alert to
everything outside her need almost a cat in dogskin
she steps sometimes with the fearing grace of a deer other
times she struts like a princess before a mirror
a fox is what it is to be alone outside your family what it is to
be absolute for a moment
her leaving is a sudden absence she leaves like breath you
don't question it you don't await its return
wherever she is there is permission she lopes through a play
of the world we yearn toward
her absence is a perfect forgetting not amnesia but the serenity
of an empty day

prayerless days

what can be made of this
an emptiness before the typer
waiting for you to enter
the animal thrashing in the lake
what can be made of the abandoned house
with its shuttered windows

there are prayerless days
in a dingy room
there are days of betrayal
when you swallow hard
human days that can't be helped

a stone plunging into water
a heap of clothes in the rain

prayer is a propping up of the corpse
a talking beyond belief
prayer is a helpless laughter

you don't know the names of things
only things themselves
what you can touch

a woman on shore is walking away
outside your window children tear the world apart with play

biography

this time van gogh gets to be born in greece
athenian light across his eyes

emily dickinson vaults the midnight horse
and gallops to her love

I'm a child in a northern tree
still climbing at the sky

hanging from the sky

with his frayed rope
a man is hanging from the sky
his mouth calls silently
his limbs shiver for a touch

what it's like to be born
at the foot of an oak
what it's like with a hundred names
and god and law and work

a man climbs into his photograph
all you see are his eyes
inside his chest a bird
and an absence in his arms

love lives in the shadow
a torn paper mask
when he leaves in the morning
she hangs up his coat

stranded in the moonlight

it's not the garden he missed nor the book
he missed the hammer
the toolbox with its clues
he missed all his father ever heard and saw

mother stepped in front of the man
the boy was hers
where his memory lived she planted dreams
he was stranded in the moonlight
cold lightning in the hills
he was a stone learning to speak

like drunks children never lie
they shift
the boy found a place
where he always told truth
beneath the foliage
his thumb in his mouth

it's not the garden he missed
but the blessing
a familiar hand in an unfamiliar world

family death

there's an end to it
lop off the tail
these shoes the old clothes
burn them

an end to solitaire on the casket
the smiling skull
the raw-boned foetus
an end to the tired story
the indulgence

living half overseas half underground
with the carnage of carthage
alpha and omega
sailing out of sleep
into the blue and red room

the house collapses
and who wouldn't?
the basement floods
and patmos sinks
this is how hallucinations end
it's how they begin

there's an end to it
no one's boy no one's man
the tattoo's been flayed
a snapshot for the album
a family gathering on the killing floor

naked as a beast
a pelt on a hook
there's an end to it or not
an old man with shattered legs
a woman without hands

and always at the centre
the family hovering
over the child's deathbed

orphan

your eyes numb from watching the blue sky
you turn to rocks and water
in the dizziness of light
you call the child from the lake
it rises white and bloated floating
face down to the deep

you embrace the child
and carry its shadow to the shore
on the beach a chair
the white leaves of a book
somewhere your empty coat
and that photograph of someone who resembles you

you are not helpless anymore
you hurl the blue bolt of an ancient war
you name the deaths and are orphaned
there's no other way
the sun's skinning you alive
and fish are flowing at your feet
it's how you make your way for a moment
across the dazzling beach

solo

do nothing she said there's nothing you can do but he's dead I
said he lay splayed on the road his mother pacing the
shoulder her face stretched across her skull he's dead
there's nothing to do she said come with me I heard the
town snoring and wind sifting through our skins

you are fatherless she said his dead watch on my wrist and
light through leaves caging my eyes I want to dance I said
like flying barefoot and light as silver I want to touch earth
for a moment

when you speak she said you move from what you know yet
god is a word you long to find the world pours out untold
stories when you are silent when your hand rests without
gesture you are godless and the world without end

if god is a dancer I understand light and levity the foot
pivoting on earth and I understand the cold sometimes
dark intrusions on spirit its capture or release how flight is
managed and ecstasy

do nothing she said god comes and goes with his clubfoot
looking for the perfect partner it's never you for more than
a moment she said he leaves you solo take heart

you're free she laughed if you want it a sad angel a ghost of
yourself a traitor I turned from the dead his mother paused
to watch something nudging her memory she raised her
pale hand and waved

godly world

worldly they say things of flesh and mind in and of this world
the body's need to touch the tongue talking ears and eyes the
smell of cabbage or skin like cloves the lick of stone the
human world of lips and arms of yellow and red with fucking
and eating and reading worldly they say the sun and wind
the world flying apart thoughts straying and horses mounting
on the shore the moon and blood a finger on the word
nothing works so the world goes on as if it means something
earth crumbling beneath us and heavens above splintering
and all the time in the world of this world and it's how you
find god in this waiting the world the godly world

the beach

the beach is littered with shoes and clothes
hats are sailing in the sky
no umbrellas and no shade
nothing here to eat but tufts of grass

a place of wind and stone
almost an empty place
the world bare-boned and remote
nothing new here nothing hidden
I see nothing but mirror inside mirror
my glass face a pool of water
there are no alibis

when the wind tears through me
and skin is a shredded coat
and this thing this hat-stand this x-ray I am
hangs against the sky
tongueless eyeless earless
what is left is this red udder this pouch my heart
drying like a fish
on the beach

this is nobody
the absence
this is god the fool
in love

abandon

you walk into the light
tall and lithe and lean

with my breath
I touch your loneliness
sometimes you welcome soft nights
there are days you turn away

I watch you empty your pockets
and disappear into the desert
I want nothing have nothing

I hold no song
it comes and goes

as for us
there is a love we can't help
there is our bravery
how we dance in and out of each other's arms

you don't get to be a saint

like stars snow's falling all over town
headlights are passing on the walls
a god's walking barefoot through the drifts

the town drunk's leaning against a tree
he sees a dead hand in the snow
and reaches down to offer his own

you don't get to be a saint the dead man says
you get to warm your hands for a moment
you get to catch your breath and say one thing

I can make you a wizard he says
I can give you life forever
but I can't take the price off your head

I don't want to be a wizard says the drunk
I live with the price and I don't mind dying
I just want to sing a lullaby

he clears his throat and sings the dead man to sleep
then he turns into stillness
like none ever heard ever more still than snow

Photo: Marijke Friesen

Patrick Friesen was born in Steinbach, Manitoba in 1946. He now lives in Winnipeg, where he is employed as a media specialist for Manitoba Education. He has written for television, film, theatre and video, and is the author of five previous books of poetry, including *The Shunning*, which he has adapted as a play. His most recent play is *The Raft*.

Also published by Turnstone Press

By Patrick Friesen:

Flicker and Hawk $8.95

The Shunning $8.95

Unearthly Horses $7.95

Other recent poetry
($8.95 each):

Di Brandt, *Agnes in the sky*

Maara Haas, *why isn't everybody dancing*

Cornelia Hoogland, *The Wire-Thin Bride*

Roy Miki, *saving face*

Patrick O'Connell, *Hoping for Angels*

Brenda Riches, *Something to Madden the Moon*

Kathleen Wall, *Without Benefit of Words*